Grab My Hand

By Gloria Gardner

Illustrations by Zellie Calavita

LUMINARE PRESS

WWW.LUMINAREPRESS.COM

Grab My Hand
Copyright © 2020 by Gloria Gardner

All rights reserved. This book or any portion thereof may not be reproduced or
used in any manner whatsoever without the express written permission of
the publisher, except for the use of brief quotations in a book review.

Printed in the United States of America

Color Illustrations by Zellie Calavita
Black and White Illustrations by Robyn Hodgdon
Cover and Interior Design by Melissa K. Thomas

Luminare Press
442 Charnelton St.
Eugene, OR 97401
www.luminarepress.com

LCCN: 2020920888
ISBN: 978-1-64388-496-7

Halloween night is so special!
It's something that we look forward to and eagerly await.
We wonder what costumes people will be wearing.
We wonder what goodies we'll get to put in our trick or treat bag.
We wonder if we'll see any of our friends.
We even wonder if there will be any surprises.
What about scary ones?
Will we hear any strange and spooky noises that might make us jump?
Could there be some scary faces that might make us shiver and quiver?
Could there be some creatures in hiding that might jump out at us?
What would we do if any of these really scary things happened?
We'd remember that a grownup was with us and could help us.
All we'd have to say is, "Grab my hand."

When it's Halloween night,
And shadows creep into sight,
Grab my hand,
And hold it tight.

When the witch with green hair
Frightens me with her glare,
Grab my hand,
I'm glad you care.

When the zombies tromp by,
And bats dart in the sky,
Grab my hand,
Don't let me cry.

When tarantulas crawl,
And skeletons rattle and fall,
Grab my hand,
I feel so small.

When monsters hammer and pound
And goblins hide all around,
Grab my hand,
Don't make a sound.

When ghosts float in the air,
And vampires give me a scare,
Grab my hand,
I need you there.

When mice scurry and squeak,
And hidden eyes peek,
Grab my hand,
I feel so weak.

When spooks moan and groan,
And wizards turn things to stone,
Grab my hand,
I feel alone.

After all the scary fun,
And our trick or treating is all done,
I can't wait to get back home.
Grab my hand, let's run, run, run!

Has anything ever scared you?
Do you wish that someone could be there
with you to grab your hand if you get scared?
Which person would you wish that would be?
Have you ever been a helper to a friend or a
little child who was afraid?
Did it help them?
How did it make you feel?

HALLOWEEN TREATS

Halloween is here, with all its scary fun.
And it's exciting that tonight we get to trick or treat.
We always like to see our goodie-bags fill up
With all the yummy candy we'll be taking home to eat.

After knocking on everyone's door,
And ringing all the doorbells on our street tonight,
It will soon be time to head back home,
And choose which piece of candy we want for our first bite.

Candy comes in different colors, different sizes, too.
Some are smooth for licking, and some you have to chew.
Licorice is really fun to bend, with its colors red or black,
And m & m's are small enough to hide inside your sack.

Candy flavors taste so good, like cherry and vanilla.
And "sugar yummies" on a stick are lollipops we like to lick.
There's also gummy worms and caramel candies, too.
These are all our favorites, the ones we like to pick.

We love the taste of jelly beans, in all their pretty colors.
And taffy chews and tutti fruttis are very, very yummy, but that's not all.
Both peanut butter candy and chocolate Kisses, too, are ones we like to choose,
And munchy-crunchies are best of all, even if they're small.

See the little candy bars, so small and snugly wrapped?
Their taste is quite delicious, so sugary and sweet.
And gumdrops and candy corn, we like these both a lot.
And when it's Halloween, we love that people give us candy for our treat!

Want to take a look at all your treats? Just spread them on the floor.
Want to know how many? Go ahead and count them, "One, two, three."
Do you think that there's enough, or do you wish for more?
With all the treats you have, you'll be happy to know there's plenty!

When Mommy says, "Bedtime, dear, it's getting late,"
I know it's time to put my treats away.
But that's okay with me, I'll hide my goodies where no one sees,
And tomorrow, I'll pretend it's Halloween again, because I really love that day!

Name Here

Your Halloween Photo Here!

Date

Made in the USA
Middletown, DE
26 September 2021

49110485R00018